MONSTER By Mistake!

One Big Sneeze

www.monsterbymistake.com

Created by
Mark Mayerson

Adapted by
Paul Kropp

Graphics by Studio 345

WINDING
STAIR
PRESS

an Imprint of Stewart House Publishing Inc.

Hi, my name is Warren.

I am just a kid like you.

One day, I was with my sister Tracy.

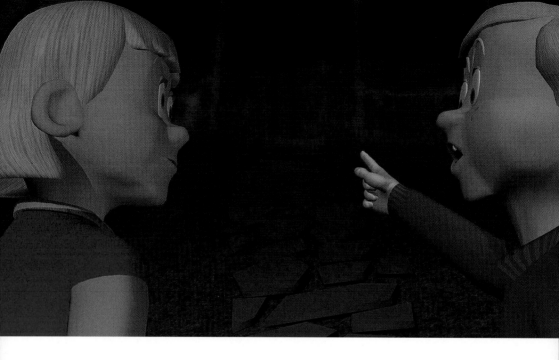

We went to an old house.

We met a little man in a glass ball.

He told us he was trapped.

He begged us to help.

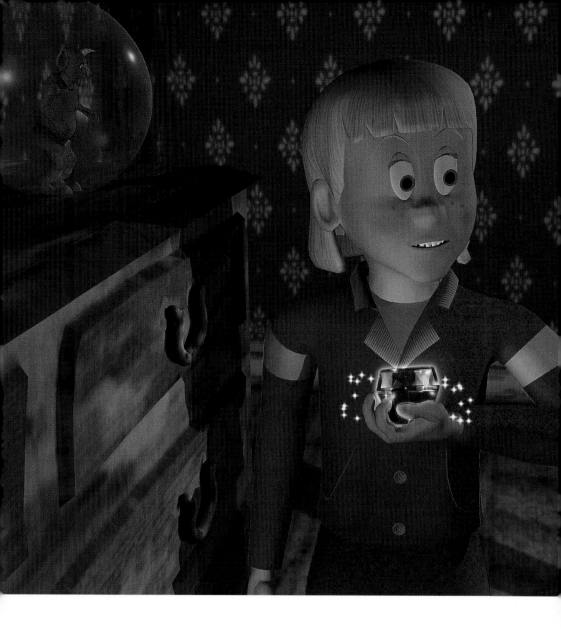

Tracy held the magic jewel.

I read the magic words.

Zap! Zip! Pow! The magic hit me.

"Are you OK?" Tracy asked.

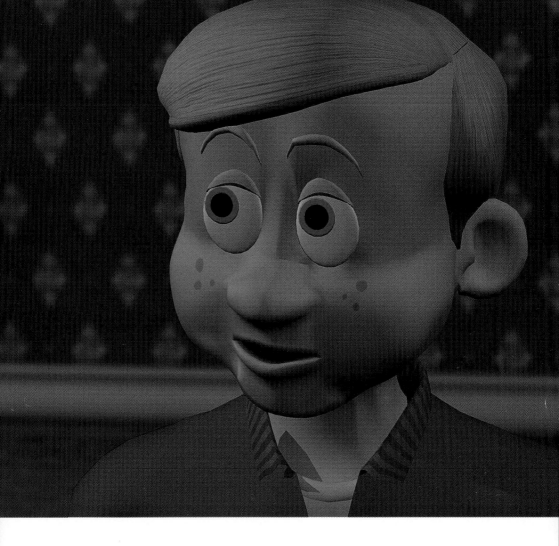

"I am fine," I told her.

The little man got mad.
"You fools!" he said.

We ran from the house.

I did a big sneeze.

Ah ... ah ... ah ... choo!

"Warren!" Tracy cried.
"You are a monster!"

"Me? A Monster?"

Then I looked at my hands.

"Oh no! I am a monster!"

"I do not want to be a monster.

I want to be a kid!"

"I have an idea," Tracy said.

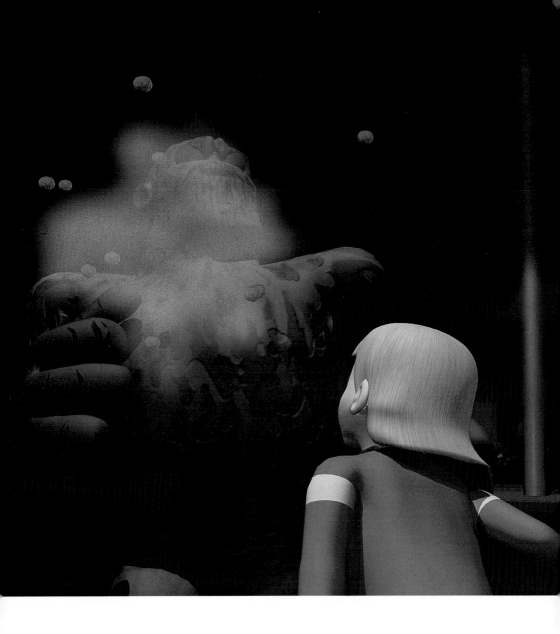

She threw dust at my face!

I did a big sneeze.

Ah ... ah ... ah ... choo!

And I was a kid!

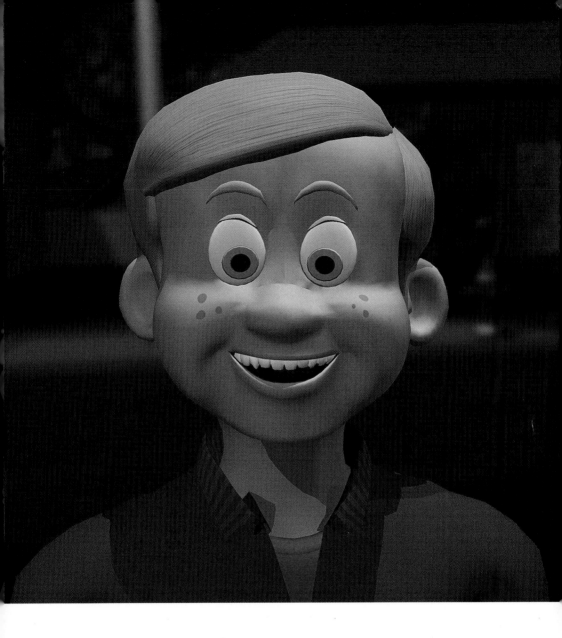

I hope I do not sneeze again!

Note to parents and teachers about Monster By Mistake Readers:

We trust your young readers will enjoy developing their reading skills with these great stories. Here is a simple guide to help you choose the right level for your child:

Level One Monster Readers
These stories are carefully written to build the confidence of beginning readers. They have been written to North American curriculum standards for Grade 1.

Featuring:
- short, simple sentences
- easy-to-recognize words
- exciting images to support the story

Level Two Monster Readers
Designed to build confidence of a new reader. They have been written to North American curriculum standards for Grade 2.

Featuring:
- slightly more difficult vocabulary
- more complex sentence and story structures
- exciting images to support the story

Level Three: Chapter books
Designed to appeal to both the advanced reader and the reluctant reader. They have been written to North American curriculum standards for Grades 3 and 4.

Featuring:
- complete plots based on the television episode
- controlled vocabulary and general readability
- stories deal with real life issues such as bullying, self-esteem and problem solving

Our Educational Consultant, Paul Kropp, is an author, editor and educator. His work includes young adult novels, novels for reluctant readers and the bestselling resource *How to Make Your Child a Reader for Life.*
Visit his website: www.paulkropp.com

Text © by Winding Stair
Graphics © 2002 by Monster By Mistake Enterprises Ltd.

Monster By Mistake Series is produced by
   CCI Entertainment Ltd. and Catapult Productions
Series Executive Producers: Arnie Zipursky and
   Kim Davidson
Based on the Screenplay "Monster by Mistake"
   by Mark Mayerson

Text Design: Counterpunch
Cover Design: Darrin La Framboise

All rights reserved.

1 2 3 4 5 6   07 06 05 04 03 02

Printed and bound in Canada

Contact Stewart House Publishing
at info@stewarthousepub.com or 1-866-474-3478

National Library of Canada Cataloguing in Publication

Mayerson, Mark
      One big sneeze / created by Mark Mayerson;
adapted by Paul Kropp.

(Monster by mistake)
Based on an episode of the television program, Monster
by mistake.
Level 1.
For use in Kindergarten to grade 1.
ISBN 1-55366-317-9

I. Kropp, Paul, 1948– II. Catapult (Firm), III. Title.
IV. Series.

PS8576.A8685O53 2002   jC813'.6   C2002-903658-5
PZ7